THE MUD LAKE TRILOGY

THE MUD LAKE TRILOGY

BY RUSSELL REECE

SHELL BRIDGE BOOKS

BETHEL, DELAWARE

Cover Art by Adrijus G. at
RockingBookCovers.com

CONTENTS

Ever run into any trouble?

THE MUD LAKE TRILOGY

BY RUSSELL REECE

THE HITCHHIKER

Just outside of Springfield, Missouri, at the remote edge of a large potato field, a man rolled a woman's body into a shallow grave alongside her detached head. He picked up the shovel but hesitated at the sight of the open eyes, the smeared lipstick smile and crushed forehead. He poked at the head with the shovel blade and then stepped into the grave and pressed down on the face with his muddy boot.

*   *   *

When Debbie wrote and said she and her parents would be visiting her uncle in Marine City, Michigan, Jeff couldn't believe his good fortune. Michigan wasn't that far away. He could arrange a long weekend liberty and with any luck make it from

3

the base in six or seven hours. They would have two-and-a-half days together. It would be incredible.

That Friday, after class, Jeff got a ride with his buddy, Termite, from Great Lakes Naval Training Center to the east side of Gary, Indiana. As the radio blared the new Stones song, (I can't get no) Satisfaction, Termite pulled his 58 Chevy off the road alongside the I94 entrance ramp. He turned down the volume. "Well, partner," Termite looked at his watch. "Any luck, you'll be banging that college girl by midnight and getting *plenty* of satisfaction."

"I told you, she's not like that."

"Oh, that's right, and you're in love." He said it again, held the vowel, "Luuuve."

"Besides, butt-head, it's her uncle's house and she's with her parents."

"That'll be fun. Have a great time with her mom and dad." Termite laughed.

Jeff pushed open the door and pulled his hat and duffle from the rear seat. "Thanks for the ride, man."

Termite made a mock salute. "Roger that, partner. Be careful."

"Always am."

As Termite drove off, Jeff smoothed the wrinkles from his white jumper and straightened his neckerchief. A hundred yards away cars whizzed by on the interstate. He put on his hat and unfolded the roadmap. I94 went east to Detroit, then turned north and passed by Marine City; one road, all the way – a four hour run.

He checked his watch; seven-thirty. Debbie and her parents were probably already there. He wondered what she might be doing right now, whether she was alone or with her relatives. And then he recalled how easy it was to be with her, how quickly she would break into a smile, or giggle. A warm feeling started inside as he lifted his bag and walked up the gravely shoulder of the entrance ramp.

He was still amazed at how close they'd become in such a short time. Both had graduated in 1963 from rival high schools in Wilmington, Delaware. She was a sophomore at Rosemont College, majoring in economics. During his two-week Christmas leave they met at a friend's party and hung out for the rest of the evening. After that, they saw each other every day and when his two-weeks were over she came to the train station with his parents. Saying goodbye had been surprisingly difficult. He had written her, expressed his wonder at those emotions, and hoped he could see her again when he was back in the fall. He was delighted when in her return letter she said she missed him and couldn't wait for his next visit. Since then they had written regularly. It was hard to believe that in a few hours he would actually be with her again.

Halfway up the entrance ramp a car approached, driven by a middle-aged woman. He held out his arm, his thumb up. The car roared by. He turned and started walking again.

Two more cars passed and then, just as he reached the top of the ramp, an older couple in a new Mustang pulled over. Jeff hustled to the car as the passenger door opened. The woman pulled her seatback forward and in a friendly voice said, "Climb on in."

Jeff checked out the driver, a balding, middle-aged gentleman with a welcoming smile, and then squeezed into the tight rear compartment. "Hey, thanks for stopping."

The man watched his mirrors and pulled back onto the interstate. "Where are you heading?"

"Marine City, north of Detroit."

"Well, we can take you as far as Watervliet. It's a little over an hour from here."

"That'll be great." Jeff set his bag on the seat next to him, stretched out and looked around the car. The tan and white leather interior gleamed and still had that new-car smell. As they reached cruising speed the driver rested his right hand on the t-bar shifter. "I've never been in a Mustang. Pretty nice," Jeff said.

"Oh, Larry had to have this car as soon as he saw it," the woman said.

The man patted his wife on the leg. "I think you like the Mustang just as much as I do, Barb."

She waved her hand in dismissal. "Oh, pooh. One car is the same as another to me."

Larry smiled at Jeff and winked. "She likes the Mustang."

Jeff settled back in his seat. Debbie worried about him hitching rides and told him so in her letters, but he brushed it off. Aside from one uncomfortable episode with a homosexual he hadn't had any problems. Even that was more of an inconvenience than anything else, but it had made him cautious. Now he did a quick survey of each driver before he got in and was prepared to step away from a car if something didn't seem right. He had done it a few months ago. The driver had seemed strange. Maybe it was the overly friendly manner, the forced smile, or the nervous hand wringing the steering wheel, he didn't really know, but the whole thing didn't feel right. So he stepped away, and interestingly enough, it had bolstered his confidence. He considered himself a pro now and trusted that his gut would keep him out of trouble.

And like any pro would do, once inside a car, Jeff watched and listened to each driver for a few minutes to figure out how he would play things, how open and honest he would be. Larry and Barb were generous with their humor and conversation. They reminded him of his Aunt Peggy and Uncle Zip, and he immediately felt at home.

"So what's your name and where are you from, son?" Larry asked.

*   *   *

An hour later, Jeff waved as the Mustang headed off the expressway toward Watervliet. He jogged past the exit ramp. The sun had gone down and the temperature had dropped noticeably from the day's eighty-degree high. Off to his right a tractor, pulling a baler and a nearly-full wagon, lumbered through a field of cut hay. He watched a man pull a bale from the chute and swing it onto the stack. As the tractor turned and started another row the driver switched on his headlights.

Jeff turned and held out his thumb. As each vehicle rushed by, blasts of hay-scented wind pelted him with sand and small pieces of debris. After several minutes, when he was beginning to wonder why the uniform had not worked its normal magic, a yellow and white, two-door Ford Fairlane pulled off the road and stopped a hundred yards away. The driver backed down the shoulder, closing the distance as Jeff ran toward the car. The driver moved a pair of muddy boots from the passenger side floor-mat and dropped them behind the seat, then nodded a greeting. He was a clean-cut guy, average build, probably in his mid-thirties. His brown hair was parted and combed over, his ironed canvas shirt tucked neatly into his jeans.

He wore a clean pair of low-top work-boots. Jeff got in. "Thanks for stopping." He took a deep breath and shoved his duffel bag on the floor under his legs.

"No problem." The driver merged onto the expressway.

Jeff glanced around the car. The back seat was filled with boxes and a crumpled-up canvas tarp. A long-handled shovel was wedged on the floor at an angle behind the front seat. The glass in the rearview mirror was broken and completely missing on one side. Small splatters of dried mud peppered the dashboard and the passenger side door. Jeff wiped the window sill with his palm to keep the dirt from getting on his white jumper. Some remained stuck to the painted surface. He dusted his hands and checked the seat for more. He had wanted to make a good impression on Debbie's relatives. The last thing he needed was to arrive in dirty clothes.

"Sorry about the mess," the driver said. "I must have missed that when I cleaned up." He slowly chewed gum. "I've been tromping around in the woods."

"I'm just glad to have a ride. My name is Jeff."

"Ted, here. Where are you heading?"

"North of Detroit. Marine City."

Ted shifted his gaze back to the road and continued to chew. "I'm going to Ann Arbor. That'll get you most of the way."

Ted spoke in a slow, mid-western accent and made few facial expressions. Not the warm and fuzzy kind, Jeff thought, but he hadn't set off any alarms either. They rode for a few miles without speaking. Jeff stared out the side-window, images of Debbie superimposed over the passing farm fields. She turned and smiled at him, pushed her shoulder-length brown hair off her cheek.

"Are you out of Great Lakes?" Ted asked.

"Yeah. I'm finishing up electronics school. Another month and I'll be done."

Ted chewed his gum. "That's a good trade. You gonna stay in the Navy?"

"No way. I'd get out tomorrow if I could."

"I did a hitch in the Army. I know where you're coming from."

"What did you do?"

"Engineer. We built roads, airstrips, stuff like that."

Jeff nodded. "Is that what you do now?"

Ted checked his mirror, glanced at Jeff and then looked back at the road. Jeff was beginning to wonder if Ted was going to answer when he finally said, "No."

It was getting dark and the dashboard lights gave an eerie glow to Ted's canvas shirt. He drove the speed limit and many cars and trucks passed them by, fully visible for a moment, eventually becoming just sets of taillights that slowly vanished in the distance.

Jeff checked his watch; nine-thirty. He wished he'd picked a faster driver.

Ted's voice broke through the quiet. "You do a lot of hitchhiking?"

"Off and on. Last time was a couple of months ago. I went up to Muskegon to visit my grandparents. It's easy when you're in uniform. You must have hitched when you were in the Army."

"I always had a car."

"Nice."

Another truck passed and then Ted asked, "Ever run into any trouble?"

Maybe it was the monotone of Ted's voice, or maybe it was just the word "trouble," but the question gave Jeff a start. He glanced at Ted who remained expressionless. "Not really. I've been picked up by queers a few times."

He immediately wished he could pull back the words. What if Ted was a homosexual? But Ted shook his head in disgust.

Relieved, Jeff continued. "When they realized I wasn't interested they usually just dropped me at the next exit and that was that. One of them got aggressive."

"What did you do?"

"I tried to be nice to the guy, but he wouldn't let it go. He kept telling me I'd like it, threatened to reach over and grab me. He wanted to know, what was the big deal? I finally told him I'd cut him if he tried. He pulled right over and I got out."

For the first time, Ted smiled.

"The only problem was I was miles from an exit, nothing around but woods, and it took a long time to get another ride. I didn't know why no one would stop until the guy that finally picked me up said he wondered if I had done something to get put out in the middle of nowhere."

Ted chewed his gum and then shifted his gaze back to Jeff. "Would you have done it?"

"What?"

"The queer, would you have cut him?"

Jeff locked eyes with Ted. It was a legitimate question, but he didn't know Ted. What did he expect him to say? His stomach tightened. "I didn't have anything to cut him with."

Jeff shifted nervously in his seat, watched the road for a few minutes and wondered if he had just said too much. It was the second time in a half-hour that he had felt uncomfortable with the conversation. Need to be more careful with this guy, he thought.

"Do they have blanket parties in the Navy?" Ted asked.

Jeff knew about blanket parties. It's where a gang of guys throw a blanket over someone, usually while they're sleeping, drag them out of bed wrapped up tight and then kick and punch the bundle. Everyone participates so no one ever sees anything. It was nothing that Jeff would want to have anything to do with. "I've heard of it; never seen it done."

"Well, when I was in we had this "friendly" guy in the troop. He walked like a god-dammed woman, sang solos in the church choir on the base." He looked at Jeff, "You know the type."

Jeff wasn't sure he wanted to hear this, but he smiled, nodded.

"Well we gave this pussy a party he would never forget. The 1st Sergeant set it up. Said he didn't want no queer-boy in his troop. They took the fag to the hospital the next day and we never saw him again. Heard they kicked him out but no one really knew." Ted shook his head. "You wonder why God makes faggots." Ted chewed slowly with his mouth open, his expression fixed in a tight sneer as if the gum had soured. Jeff looked away, glad this acquaintance would be over in hour or so.

Another large truck lumbered by, a tattered University of Michigan pennant flapping angrily from the side mirror. The exit sign for Battle Creek came into view then passed. More than halfway, he thought. He imagined standing with Debbie, their arms entwined as she looked up into his face wearing that peaceful, loving smile. A couple more hours.

"You from Marine City?"

"No, I'm just meeting up with my girlfriend for a long weekend."

"Oh yeah, what's her name?"

"Debbie."

"*Debbie.*" How long have you and *Debbie* been hanging around together?"

Jeff chafed at Ted's emphasis of the name. "I met her at a party when I was home at Christmas. We've been writing almost every day." Jeff paused, thought of the beige envelopes and stationary, the flowing, feminine handwriting.

"You've got to watch out for women," Ted finally said. "There aren't many good ones."

"She's a good one alright."

Ted stared forward. In a quiet, measured voice he said, "Well, you're a lucky man."

Jeff checked for a ring but Ted's left hand was curled around the steering wheel. "You married?"

Ted's jaw tightened and his eyes appeared to glaze. After a long pause, he said, "My wife died."

"Oh, sorry." Jeff felt awkward, but also somewhat relieved. Maybe Ted's strange nature came from struggling with the loss of his wife.

"She was a self-centered bitch who had no respect for anyone, especially me." He checked his side mirror. "It couldn't have happened to a nicer person."

Jeff stiffened in his seat. He felt as if he had just been spun in a circle. And now he had a million questions running through his head, but Ted was such a weird bird he wasn't about to ask any of them.

Fortunately, Ted would be out of his life in another hour or so.

Just east of Jackson, Ted flipped on the blinker. "I've got to get some gas, hit the head. There's a station up here."

Jeff nodded. "Good. I could use a pit stop." And a break from you, he thought.

At the Ann Arbor Road Gas and Go, Ted pulled behind a pickup at the crowded pumps. "Go ahead. I'll fill her up and park over there." He pointed at a series of open spaces.

Jeff got out and went inside the busy station. The small restroom had two urinals, two stalls and a long line. He waited his turn, used the urinal, then worked through the crowd of men to the sink. As he washed away the dirt from Ted's car, the water in the bowl turned pinkish-brown. He grabbed a paper towel and dried his hands, then checked his uniform sleeves and twisted his shoulders in front of the mirror to insure the dirt hadn't soiled the back of his jumper or pants. He wanted Debbie to be proud when she saw him. An old man standing in the crowd said, "Come on buddy, we ain't got all day here."

"Sorry," Jeff said. He moved away from the sink and tossed the towel.

On his way out of the restroom, Ted walked in. "I'll be right there."

Jeff nodded and for a moment toyed with the idea of finding another ride. It would be a hassle but he could do it. Then he realized his duffel-bag was locked in Ted's car. So much for that, he thought.

He glanced at the magazine rack and then went outside. It was a dark night but the parking lot was well lit and filled with travelers. He leaned on Ted's fender and watched a family, with a little boy and a pretty teenage girl, load into a station-wagon with Delaware plates.

He stretched and thought about Debbie. Less than two hours now and they would be together. He thought of that last night at the train station when he had returned to Great Lakes, how her voice had trembled when she said goodbye and how her hug had seemed more real than any hug he had ever had before. Even now he could smell the faint note of spearmint in her hair, feel her fuzzy coat-collar tickling his face and her hands tight on the pit of his back. It had all been so unexpected.

He looked toward the station just as Ted came down the stairs and started across the lot. "It's open," he said.

Jeff tried the door, then mentally chided himself as he moved his duffle-bag and slipped inside.

Ted pulled open the driver-side door and something heavy and metallic fell to the concrete. Ted picked up a twenty-inch piece of steel pipe, slipped it onto the floor, then got in the car. His blank expression met Jeff's questioning gaze, held for several seconds, then dissolved into a phony smile. He started the engine, pulled out of the lot and back onto the interstate.

Ted stared forward, trancelike, his lips parted. Jeff turned and looked out his side window, his mind raced. What was Ted doing with a steel pipe? He glanced at the splatters on the dashboard and windowsill, rubbed one with his finger. A vision of the pinkish water in the sink flashed in his mind. He looked at the broken mirror and back to the splatters. *Ever run into any trouble?* A chill coursed through him.

He checked his watch again, then picked up his duffle and rested it on his lap. He pulled out the map and in as nonchalant a voice as possible said, "That was Jackson back there, right?" His hands shook as he imagined the cold pipe smacking someone in the face, blood splattering.

Ted didn't respond. He continued to stare forward, his face occasionally illuminated in the headlights of oncoming cars.

"Well, if that was Jackson, I figure we're less than an hour to Ann Arbor." Jeff struggled to refold the map and then slipped it back into the duffle. He left the bag on his lap, rested his arms on top.

Ted reached into his shirt pocket and pulled out a stick of gum. Jeff watched him slip the stick into his mouth and crumble the shiny foil.

Debbie. Jeff closed his eyes and took a deep breath. He was so close, and every minute that passed he got closer. But Debbie seemed a million miles away now – a tiny smiling face at the end of an inverted telescope.

An eighteen-wheeler churned past. Ted chewed with his mouth open. Jeff smelled the sweet gum and his stomach turned. He shifted in his seat until he was cattycorner between the seatback and the door. From this vantage point he could inconspicuously keep his eye on Ted. Maybe it's all my imagination, he thought. But then he recalled Ted's glee over the blanket party...his dead wife. A drip of sweat ran down the back of Jeff's neck. Why hadn't he gotten out of the car back at the gas station?

Ted moved his leg and looked down on the floor. The pipe had rolled forward and lay against his heel. He reached down, picked it up.

Jeff felt a wash of horror as Ted placed the pipe across his lap. His grip tightened around the steel before he released it and moved his hand back to the steering wheel. Ted's face lit up from headlights, went dark again.

Jeff gripped both sides of his duffel-bag. His voice cracked at the edges as he said, "What's the pipe for, Ted?"

Ted's expression hardened and the hardness seemed to project through his body, into his arms and legs.

"What's the pipe for?" Jeff's voice was stronger this time. He tightened his grip on the duffle, prepared to fend off any blow that might come his way.

Ted looked at him, then turned his gaze back to the road. "I use it in my work," he said.

Jeff felt a sliver of relief. But then the small face at the end of the telescope seemed to fade and Jeff's mouth went dry. He tried to swallow. "What kind of work do you do?"

Ted stopped chewing. "You writing a book?" His hand moved from the steering wheel and wrapped around the end of the pipe. He took a deep breath and looked back at Jeff.

Another car passed. Jeff glanced out his side-window and then back to Ted. "Pull over and let me out," Jeff said.

Ted didn't respond and in the wash of oncoming headlights Jeff noticed the hint of a smile. Ted released his grip on the pipe and rested his hand on the gearshift. "What's the problem? We'll be in Ann Arbor in forty-five minutes."

"You're freaking me out with the pipe. Pull over. Please."

Ted laughed. He mimicked Jeff's shaky voice, "Please." Then his expression grew distant and soured. Under his breath he said, "Please. That always fixes everything." He rolled down his window and spit out the gum. "It's the middle of nowhere," he said. "You told me before; no one's going to want to pick you up out here."

"That's my problem. Pull over."

Ted kept the car at sixty.

"Surveyor."

"What?"

"You asked what kind of work I do. I'm a surveyor. I work for a lumber company that owns property throughout the Midwest."

Surveyor, – the pipe, the muddy boots, the shovel – that would make sense. Jeff's head reeled. Maybe it was all his imagination.

"I make sure the local crew's lines are on the up-and-up. When you own as much land as we do, you wouldn't believe how often the hometown boys try to carve away a sliver here or there." He paused for a moment and a devilish smile appeared. "You can't trust people today."

Jeff stared at the pipe, not sure what to say. He felt foolish but at the same time still very frightened.

Ted continued, "I use pipes for markers. Pound 'em in and spot 'em with orange spray-paint. There's a box of them in the trunk."

Jeff said nothing. He shifted in his seat and relaxed his grip on the duffle.

"When I cleaned up at the last job-site I missed one. I saw it when I was changing my boots and just stuck it in the car." Ted looked at Jeff again and then back to the road. "Why? You think I'm going to use it on you?" Ted laughed.

"I don't know. I just got freaked, I guess. Sorry."

Ted continued to laugh and soon Jeff was smiling and shaking his head. Ted swung his empty right hand and pantomimed hitting Jeff with the pipe. As his arm straightened near Jeff's forehead Ted clicked his tongue. "Got ya, sailor boy."

Jeff was embarrassed now and grew more so as Ted continued to laugh. Ted pantomimed hitting him again and then did it a third time, the tongue clicks replaced with Ted repeating the word, "Thunk, thunk."

Jeff laughed, but was getting tired of playing and his embarrassment was changing to annoyance. "Alright, Ted. I get your point."

They passed a "Men Working" sign where an arrow and pylons directed traffic into the right lane. Ted reduced speed as cars and trucks formed into a single line. He continued to laugh and then his fingers tapped Jeff's forehead. "Thunk." Flashing lights showed in the distance.

Jeff swatted at Ted's hand, but missed. "That's enough," he said. The line of traffic grew slower as they approached a brightly-lit overpass under construction. In front of them a flagger held a "Slow" sign and motioned with his down-turned palm.

Ted's fingers touched Jeff's head again. "Thunk."

Jeff grabbed Ted's wrist. "Knock it off, Ted. This is getting weird." He pushed Ted's arm away.

Ted's smile faded and his right hand wrapped around the end of the pipe. His muscles tensed as if to swing but then his gaze caught on the flagger and he froze.

Jeff pushed himself tight against the door and grabbed his duffel with both hands. "Let go of the pipe, Ted!" The car slowed again.

"You little piss-ant." Ted's face glowed from the lights at the overpass worksite. He shifted his gaze to Jeff, then quickly back to the car in front of them. He stomped on his brake to avoid a collision. "You get in my car and then you want to fucking run things." Ted watched the car in front but then turned and poked the pipe toward Jeff who nervously shielded himself with the duffle bag. Ted hit the brake and the tires chirped as they passed the flagger. "You don't tell me what to do. No one tells me what to do."

They were down to twenty and going single file. Concrete barriers lined the edge of the road and on the other side construction workers jack-hammered the highway surface. Just beyond the barriers the car in front of them bounced onto a set of steel plates. Ted hit the brake again then turned his red face toward Jeff, gritted his teeth. "Where do you come off getting rough with me? Huh?"

In a quick glance Jeff saw the leading car clear the plates and begin to accelerate. He only had a moment. Ted was still facing him as their front tires thumped onto the plates. Jeff pointed and screamed, "Watch out!"

Ted slammed on the brake. Jeff pushed open the door and fell backwards onto the gravel apron. He slid a few feet on his backside, his duffel-bag flopping next to him. Ted's car bounced onto the highway with a deep metallic clank.

The interior light illuminated Ted's angry face until he accelerated and the door slammed shut. Jeff sat in the road and dusted his skinned hands as the Ford's round taillights faded into the darkness. He closed his eyes as a welcome sense of relief washed over him, but then he grew nauseous as he realized just how bad it could have been.

Running footsteps approached and a guy in a blue bump-hat shouted, "Hey man, are you okay?"

Jeff got up as several construction workers approached. He dusted off his pants and the back of his jumper. The steel plate continued to clank as cars bounced onto the highway. His hands stung and his stomach was queasy, but at least he hadn't broken anything. Not so lucky with his white uniform though. "Yeah. I'm good. Just glad to get away from that weirdo."

"What did he do?" Another guy asked.

"He was coming at me with a piece of pipe."

"You ought to call it in, man. We got a mobile radio over at the truck."

Jeff thought for a moment, imagined the delay as the police questioned him. They certainly wouldn't let him back on the road to thumb again. He might never get to Marine City. And besides, Ted could say he didn't do anything. What did he do, really? As cars and trucks rolled past, that question hit Jeff like a heavy stone.

He shook his head. "Naw, I'd just get busted for hitchhiking."

"Suit yourself, man." The group of workers started back to the overpass. The guy with the blue hat pointed at him. "Be careful."

Jeff nodded. He thought he had been careful.

The guy followed the others back to the job.

Jeff picked up his bag and walked a few hundred feet beyond the overpass, all the while replaying the encounter with Ted. What had he missed?

He turned and stuck out his thumb. Within five minutes an old pickup truck with Missouri plates pulled over. Jeff could hear blue-grass music before he opened the door. The driver was in his forties, wearing a Cardinals baseball cap, a long-sleeved shirt and rumpled khaki pants. He smiled, reached forward and turned down the radio. "Hop on up here, young fellow." The driver picked up a Bible from the seat and slid it onto the dashboard.

"Thanks for stopping," Jeff said. He didn't see the shovel in the back, or the straight-razor the man had tucked alongside his leg.

ABRACADABRA

The last 24 hours had been a tumbling blur of headlights, road signs and toll booths. Wallace had been swept up in it all, not caring where he went, just rolling with the flow of traffic as his mind raced over images of Rhonda in the foyer, holding her open lipstick and looking at him standing next to her in the reflection of the mirror. *"Just what is it that you do, Wallace? How do you contribute to this household?"* she asked. He smelled her perfume; saw her white, silk blouse, her tailored, navy blue business suit and the familiar stern gaze. He looked at himself, a rumpled, balding man, an inch shorter than Rhonda in her heels, with his usual hangdog expression, but also with the hammer this time. Rhonda glared. *"You and your Bible and your ridiculous church. You're pathetic."* She leaned forward and applied the lipstick. He was used to her criticism. It was something that

came with living with a strong woman. He had
learned that from his mother. But then he saw himself
whack Rhonda in the side of her forehead, heard her
whine as she crumpled onto the floor. He heard the
floorboards creak as he, catlike, went down on his
knees and delivered a final blow. All this repeated
again and again in the moving frenzy of the interstate,
of truck wheels turning, of red taillights glowing in the
night. He glanced at the heavy silver necklace
dangling from his rear view mirror and felt a chill. He
couldn't let himself think about that now. He couldn't.

He crossed into Michigan and drove for
another hour. The sign ahead said Jackson. He was
tired. He pulled into the first motel he came to.

*   *   *

From his window-booth in the diner Wallace
closed his Bible and watched two thirty-something
waitresses in pink uniforms take a smoke break. The
mousy brunette leaned on the counter and twisted a
strand of hair as she listened to the blonde, with the
Marilyn Monroe hairdo, complain about her
boyfriend. The blonde held her cigarette at ear level
and puffed between dramatic gestures and rapid-fire
speech. She finally pointed toward the parking lot.
"Any day now he's going to pull into the lot and that'll
be it. I gotta get out of here." The brunette picked a
flake of tobacco off her tongue and nodded.

The blonde caught Wallace's gaze and put her cigarette in the shared ashtray. She picked up a pot of coffee and headed to his table. "Everything okay here, hon?" She topped off the thick ceramic cup. "So what brings you out at three o'clock in the morning?"

He motioned through the window at the ramshackle motel across the road. "I don't sleep well in strange beds," he said.

"There's never much sleeping going on over there." She picked up his dirty plate. "It's just an in-and-out place, if you know what I mean." She glanced at the Bible. "You ready for the check?"

"Yeah, I'll take it."

She pulled her order-pad and a pencil from the pocket of her apron. Wallace shifted his gaze out the window. A car with two occupants backed out of the motel parking lot and disappeared down the deserted highway. His truck and an old sedan a few spaces away were the only vehicles left in the lot. He slowly moved his fingers in a small circle on the tabletop and recalled the car that had almost come to a stop yesterday morning as he pulled out of the potato field outside of Springfield, Missouri, the man and woman inside the car straining to see him. They could have gotten his number, identified his truck. The police might already be involved.

The waitress slid the check onto the table. "Take your time, honey." She smiled and turned away.

He pulled out his wallet, sorted through bills and took out a ten. He grabbed the check and started to slide out of the booth but then stopped. At the edge of the counter the blonde looked into a mirrored compact and touched up her lipstick. He drew a deep breath. He saw Rhonda lying on the floor, eyes wide open, fresh lipstick smeared across her cheek, and for a moment he was overcome again with the same tingling rush he had felt that afternoon as he hovered over Rhonda's body.

The blonde slipped the makeup back into a patent leather purse and shoved it under the counter.

He shook it off, slid from the booth and walked to the register.

The brunette slouched behind the glass-topped counter and took his check. "That's $5.85." She speared the check onto a wire post.

"Give me a pack of those Lifesavers," he said.

She reached under the counter, pointed with her nail-bitten finger. "Which do you want?"

"The Cryst O Mints."

"Ugh. Too strong for me," she said as she slid the roll toward him. She pushed on the register keys with both hands. "Total is $6.15."

He handed her the ten and she counted out his change. He returned to the booth, dropped a single, then picked up the cup and drained the remaining coffee.

The blonde walked up alongside him. "Be glad to get you more."

Without looking at her, he shook his head no, picked up his Bible and headed toward the entrance.

"Thanks," she said. She slipped the bill into her apron pocket. "Come see me again, honey."

As he crossed the deserted highway, he opened the roll of mints and popped one of the clear candies in his mouth. It was a crisp, summer night and the fresh air was a nice compliment to the sweet menthol flavors erupting over his taste buds. He fingered the large plastic fob on his room key.

At the diner with other people around, he had been able to control himself, to push the thoughts away and read his Bible. But he knew when he was alone in his room he would relive every second, from the moment Rhonda collapsed onto the floor until he piled on the last shovelful of dirt in the potato field. And he would recall the first time when he killed the soldier, the amazing adrenaline rush that came after he pulled the man into the alley, the sense of power, and the surprising feelings of arousal that he experienced for weeks after. How he had succumbed to those feelings, again and again, just as he had begun to do now after killing Rhonda. He shook his head, wondered what made him do that.

He looked across the road at the diner. Through the window he could see the two waitresses standing by the counter, smoking. He pulled out his truck keys, opened the door and got inside. Maybe a ride would calm him. He started the engine and sat there tapping his fingers on the wheel, listening to the muffler burble. He poked at the necklace, watched it swing back and forth. He could see it slipping off Rhonda's headless torso and he fought to contain a smile. He backed out of the lot and headed north.

He hadn't meant to kill Rhonda. He had been working on the porch step and had come inside to get a broom. Somehow it just happened. It had been the same with the soldier twenty years earlier. The guy had been drunk and staggered into him in a parking lot outside a bar. The soldier started mouthing off about how he could take care of himself, wasn't afraid of anyone. Weaving on his feet, the guy pulled out a straight-razor, waved it in the air, and then, based on some bizarre, booze infused logic, placed the razor in Wallace's hand, patted it as if to make it disappear, and then turned and started to stumble away. Wallace never even thought about it. He reached across the soldier's shoulder and slit the man's throat. There was no remorse, no guilt. He even kept the razor as a souvenir.

Wallace switched on the radio and immediately lowered the volume on the bluegrass music that blasted through the speakers. He needed to think. The two-lane road was empty and dark but for an occasional southbound vehicle. He slipped another mint into his mouth.

Maybe if he hadn't killed that soldier it might have been different with Rhonda. She was eleven years older than he and had worked with his mother at the bus company before leaving to get into real estate. When his mother died he fell apart and Rhonda took charge of things, helped him through it. He admired her strong character and forthright manner and one thing led to another. They had been married thirteen years and though Rhonda could be bossy and wanted nothing to do with the church, it had been a decent relationship. She became a successful broker. Wallace looked up to her. Then the plant closed and he lost his job in the mail room. There was nothing else in town. He wanted to move but she was making a lot of money and made it clear they weren't going anywhere. He spent his time keeping the house and doing maintenance work at the church.

Rhonda worked him over about it every chance she got. *"If I wanted a housekeeper I could do a lot better than you,"* she would say. He didn't mind. He tried to joke about it, find ways to please her. But then came the late evening business meetings, the phone calls she took in another room, her cold, amused stares when he got up the nerve to ask her about them.

Well... Rhonda wasn't so high and mighty anymore.

In the distance he could see the flashing lights of a stopped police cruiser. He checked his speed. His gut tightened as he approached. In the cruiser's headlights a female officer was conducting a sobriety check on a skinny, long-haired teenager with no shirt. Wallace grinned as he passed by.

There hadn't been any issues after he killed the soldier. It had been late at night, they'd been alone and it was just a coincidence he was walking by the bar. There was a blurb on the news; that was all.

He was still living at home and his only worry was that his mother might find out. He was uneasy around her for weeks. She always seemed to be able to read his mind, would know whenever he had done something wrong. And even though he was twenty at the time she would slap and scold him, take away privileges. *"You're still living in my house, you will obey my rules."* He wilted under his mother's attacks, would abide her cruel punishments and then pray with her. He worked hard for redemption and received such joy in her forgiveness. She never suspected a thing. It was the first time in his life he had been able to keep a secret from her and he was convinced that God had answered his prayers.

Things were different this time. Rhonda wasn't a drunken soldier stumbling through a dark parking lot in urban St. Louis where the potential for murder lurked around every corner. She was a well-known business woman. Someone would wonder why she hadn't shown up for her appointment, would try to contact her. Eventually they would come looking. He didn't want to deal with that.

Now it was 4:00 am and he was in the small town of Waterloo. Traffic was light. He passed a 7-Eleven where a group of construction workers with bags of fast food and large Styrofoam containers of coffee were getting back into a rusty, oversized pickup truck. A town police cruiser was parked against the building. Through the window Wallace saw a cop with a huge belly leaning on the counter stirring his coffee, talking with a female clerk with long blonde hair.

Wallace turned south and drove past Mud Lake and the Waterloo Recreation Area. Maybe he could say he had just gone fishing for a few days. People knew he did that from time to time. He could say she'd been at home when he left, he had no idea where she was. He thought of the couple who saw him coming out of the field. That could be a problem.

He glanced at the Bible lying on the seat next to him. His faith had saved him the first time and he knew it was his answer now. A couple days of prayer and he would know what to do. He had the time. He doubted the police were looking for him. And even if they were, what's the chance they would find him at a ratty motel in Michigan?

*　　*　　*

He put Rhonda's head on a moonlit stump and fixed up her hair with his fingers. He sat down in front of the stump, elbows on his knees, chin on his clenched-together hands. He turned the head slightly so they were face to face. Rhonda's eyelids drooped.

"You look tired," he said.

He reached into his shirt pocket, took out a roll of lifesavers, slipped one into his mouth. He studied the contours of Rhonda's face, her high cheekbone and full lips. The silver hoop earrings he had given her for Christmas glimmered in the soft light. She had always been a pretty woman. "I didn't plan to do it," he said. He shifted the candy around with his tongue. "The Lord's hand was in it. I know you're not a believer, but we are just His instruments." He glanced at Rhonda's torso lying next to the half-dug grave, took a breath between clenched teeth and unconsciously stroked himself through his pants.

He stood up, paced back and forth in front of the stump. "I loved being your husband, Rhonda. Even the last few months when you had to go out so much at night I was okay. Oh, I knew what you were doing. I knew. I prayed about it and I was okay. I was still proud to be with you.

"It wasn't my doing," he said. He sat down in front of the stump, picked up a handful of small dirt clods and tossed them one by one at Rhonda's face. It was times like this that he missed his mother most.

*   *   *

Wallace was still driving through the countryside in the hazy grey light of early morning. He passed through a wooded area under a canopy of towering maple and poplar trees and past a farm with cattle lying in the field. Near the edge of a misty meadow he spotted a one-room clapboard church that seemed as if it was from another time. The neat black and white sign by the road read, The Church of the Holy Redeemer. He pulled into the parking lot.

Wallace got out of the truck with his Bible and tried the door but it was locked. He walked down the sidewalk into an adjacent cemetery separated from the meadow by a low brick wall. The graves nearest the church had simple sandstone markers, many from the 1800's but as he walked further the stones were newer and more elaborate. Near the wall he found a memorial with a tall, granite cross and a plaque containing the script, "With the guidance of the Holy Spirit."

Wallace knelt down. With both hands, he raised the Bible to the cross and closed his eyes. "I am forever your servant, Lord."

He hugged the Bible against his chest and stared at the grey sky. "I was a foolish man. I believed Rhonda's heart was pure, like mother's. I would have done anything for Rhonda. But you knew better. You knew, and your justice was swift."

Wallace lowered his eyes. "And Lord, forgive me, but I am now filled with arrogant pride. I should be humbled to have been your servant, but, it's like the other time, Lord. I feel such joy, such passion." He swallowed. "And it manifests in disgusting, worldly ways. I've tried to stop, but I can't." He raised his eyes. "Help me Lord. I'm so ashamed."

And then the morning sun broke over the horizon and the cross was surrounded by a golden halo that seemed to grow in intensity before Wallace's eyes. His jaw dropped; his heart beat wildly. He thrust his Bible-clenched hands toward the cross and felt the Holy Spirit fill his body. When he thought he might burst he began to jerk uncontrollably and from his tongue and from deep within his soul, came a rolling tumble of glorious sounds spoken in the perfect language of the Lord.

*   *   *

As he drove back to the motel, Wallace was elated. The Lord had spoken to him. He didn't have to worry anymore. The Lord would protect him. The Lord would provide for his needs. And Wallace would be available, would serve whenever he was called. His hand would be guided by the supreme power.

He was tired, but suddenly hungry. He stopped at the convenience store at Waterloo. The female clerk he had seen earlier this morning was still on duty and she smiled at him as he came through the door. "Morning, Sweetie," she said.

He nodded, looked her over with a purpose he had never felt before. He smiled back and then spotted the ice-cream cooler. He bought a Klondike Bar and sat down on the curb in front of the store, peeled back the shiny wrapper and took a bite. A banged up truck with a Sal's Driveway Coating, Inc. logo on the side pulled in and parked against the curb several feet away. Two twenty-something guys in dirty jeans and sweatshirts got out and hustled toward the door. "Get me a pack of cigarettes," one said. "I've got to hit the head."

Wallace checked them out like a cop on the beat.

* * *

Wallace slept for twelve hours, his best sleep in several days. He dreamed about the night in the potato field, how he had dug the grave with Rhonda's tarp-covered body lying nearby. He had intended to just push the bundle in but as he dug he thought of the startled expression that remained on her face and he felt aroused. He wanted to see her again so he wouldn't forget any of the details. He un-wrapped the tarp until the body was nearly freed, then yanked with both hands like a magician unveiling a trick. The tarp, still grasped in his right hand, fluttered off to the side.

In his dream it seemed so funny. He covered the body and ripped the tarp off again. "Abracadabra," he said and laughed. He looked at Rhonda's stony face, her partially shut eyelids, eyeballs gleaming in the moonlight. He kneeled down next to her and poked at the wound on her forehead. "Does that hurt?" he said. He stared at her for a long time and then stroked himself, shuddered. He ran his finger over the contours of Rhonda's face, down her chin and across her neck. And he thought of the soldier and the first time when he had reached across the man's shoulder and slit his throat, the gagging sounds, how the blood had gushed and splattered on the ground, how he had been consumed by that moment so many times alone in his bedroom, masturbating quietly, afraid of waking his mother down the hall. He knew the punishment if she found out what he was doing, had suffered it before, each time more severe and embarrassing, but he couldn't help himself so he was quiet and when the blissful moment passed he prayed, asked God's forgiveness for disobeying his mother.

But his mother was gone and he had confessed to God and God had shined on him and called him into His service. Everything was as it should be now. In his dream he watched himself slip the razor from his pocket, open the blade and drag it lightly across Rhonda's windpipe. In the moonlight a thin line appeared. He did it again and a little blood seeped along the length of the cut. He tried to calm his breathing as he smeared the blood across her neck with his thumb but his adrenaline was pumping. He felt her throat with his hand, probed the muscle, cartilage and soft tissue like a doctor checking a thyroid. In the soft spot just below her left ear Wallace pressed in the angular tip of the razor and drew it hard and deep across her throat. Her neck gaped open and there was blood but not the gush he had expected. He sliced again and Rhonda's head tilted awkwardly away from her body. The razor caught on cartilage and her vertebrae. And now, in his dream he saw Rhonda's partially severed head in the moonlight and the subsequent strokes with the razor as he doggedly worked until the head came free and the necklace slipped off and pooled onto the ground in a shiny puddle. He woke up, his penis hard and tingly. He lay there in bed, eyes closed in half sleep, images of the dream and the moonlit night coming and going.

"Abracadabra," he said.

* * *

Wallace had a late dinner of steak, green-beans and potatoes at the diner. He was finishing up when the blonde waitress hustled in to start her shift. She stashed her purse and was quickly tying on her apron when a surly-looking cook opened the kitchen door, glanced at the clock and then called her in with his wagging finger.

41

"Sorry, Tony," she said as she went through the door. "I had a dead battery. I had to get one of the neighbors to start my car." The door closed as Tony's gruff voice took over the conversation.

Wallace picked up his Bible and his ticket and went to the cash register. The brunette that had checked him out the night before gave him another pack of Lifesavers and took his money but then looked up at her friend who had come out of the kitchen. The brunette's eyes widened. "Did he can ya?" she said.

The blonde brushed the question away with a swipe of her hand. "Pfff. Tony's a pussycat," she said. She turned toward Wallace and smiled. "Thought you'd be long gone by now." The brunette closed the register door, handed Wallace his change and went to wait on another customer.

"I'll be around a couple more days," he said.

The blonde nodded. "I'll keep the coffee warm."

Wallace went back to his room, stretched out on his bed, peeled open the Lifesavers and slipped two of the candies in his mouth. He switched on the TV, flipped through the local channels. The Tigers - Cubs game was in the last inning. A few minutes later he checked his watch – 9:30 pm. He turned off the TV, grabbed his keys and Bible.

It was a warm night and the sky was clear and bright. He drove slowly through the countryside with his window open, his arm resting on the jamb. He stuck his hand out and let the rushing air press against his open palm. It was fresh and made him feel alive. He didn't know where he was going, or what he would do but he wasn't worried anymore. He just had to be ready whenever he was called. And he would be.

He turned on the radio already tuned to the local bluegrass station. Wade Mariner and the Sons of the Mountaineers started into the song, "Anywhere is Home." It was one of Wallace's favorites and given his current circumstances, prophetic. Another message, he thought, another confirmation from the Lord. He hummed along.

He had been driving for an hour when he approached the turn to I94. He knew he would pass the motel if he took the interstate west. The Foggy Mountain Boys sang "Crying My Heart Out Over You." Wallace pulled onto the entrance ramp. He had gone four miles when he came to a series of pylons and a lighted construction area. He slowed the pickup. As he approached the flagger and clanked over a large piece of steel covering a hole in the road, he noticed several hard-hatted workers gathered on the side of the eastbound lane. In the middle of the group was a sailor in his white uniform, dusting himself off. *That was odd.* He watched as long as he could, cleared the work-area and continued down the interstate. Something wasn't right. He drove on but it kept niggling at him. He had to go back.

He made a U-turn at a crossover and sped toward the construction zone. He slowed the truck and strained to see. The men were all at work and the sailor was gone. Maybe he had been confused. Maybe it had just been some kind of weird vision. His hands wrung on the steering wheel. He couldn't remember when he had felt so unsettled. A car behind him honked. Wallace accelerated. Just beyond the work area the car sped past him.

And then in the distance, illuminated by headlights, the sailor walked along the side of the road. As the pickup approached he turned and held out his thumb.

Wallace made it a point to never pick up hitchhikers. He had even braved an argument with Rhonda about it once. "You just never know what could happen," he had said. Now, in the dark, and in the wash of the headlights the sailor's white uniform gave an otherworldly glow. Wallace felt his adrenaline pump as he passed by and although he hadn't planned to do it, he pulled the pickup off the road and stopped on the gravel apron. The sailor jogged to the truck. Wallace watched in his rearview mirror and felt a strange calm come over him.

The sailor pulled open the passenger door. Wallace turned down the music. "Hop on up here, young fellow," Wallace said. He took the Bible off the seat and slid it onto the dashboard.

The sailor glanced at Wallace and then at the Bible. He got in and closed the door. "Thanks for stopping," he said.

*   *   *

"Can't sleep again?" the waitress said as she topped off Wallace's coffee. It was 2:00 am and the diner only had one other patron.

Wallace looked up from his Bible. "I'm getting ready to turn in now."

The waitress glanced at the book. "You a preacher?"

"No, not a preacher," he said.

The waitress looked at him as if she was expecting more.

For the first time since he had come into the diner Wallace noticed the woman's nametag pinned to her lapel. "I'm just a servant of the Lord, Loraine," he said.

She hesitated. "Well, that's nice. Good for you."

Wallace walked back to the motel. In his room he stood in front of the mirror over the bureau. He leaned forward and checked his teeth in the reflection, then inspected the red streaks in his eyes. The razor and silver necklace lay on top of the bureau next to his keys and a half-eaten pack of Lifesavers. He absent-mindedly spun the razor like a top and tapped his fingers on the bureau until it stopped spinning. He pulled open the bureau drawer and took out the sailor's white-hat, put it on his head, and pushed the hat forward at a smartass cocky angle. He turned sideways, smiled at himself, saluted.

WHAT SHE WANTED

Just after 4:00 am, on the way home from her job at the diner, Loraine turned onto Big Pine Road and noticed a junky old Chevy parked on the gravel apron near the intersection. As she drove by, the headlights flipped on and the old car pulled out behind her. She heard it accelerate, checked her rearview mirror, thought it would pass, but the car slowed down and began to follow. She watched the headlights, wondered who would be out at this time of the morning, and then the engine roared and the car raced forward. Just as it seemed about to crash into her she screamed, but the driver hit the brakes and the car backed off, the engine popping and splattering behind her. Frightened now, Loraine turned onto Ridge Road toward the trailer she rented. She watched her mirror, felt her heart sink when the

Chevy made the same turn. She sped up but the car came charging toward her again, weaving erratically from side to side. "Go on by," she said, but for more than a mile the car followed. It was often so close its headlights were blocked from her view and as they passed a lighted warehouse, Loraine caught the silhouette of a single driver, thin, with wild, tousled hair that seemed translucent at the edges. "Oh God, Mickey," she whispered. Then the car rammed her and she lurched forward and struggled to retain control. In the distance, headlights approached. The Chevy slammed her again and accelerated, pushing her to the center of the road. Loraine stood on her brakes; the Chevy slid off the rear bumper. Her car fishtailed and crossed into the path of an oncoming pickup truck. She missed a collision by inches, clipped a telephone pole, spun around and stopped against a fence. The Chevy roared on down the road. The pickup pulled onto the shoulder and stopped.

As the sound of the menacing engine faded, Loraine leaned against the steering wheel, her heart pounding, her mind trying to calm the frenzy of the last few minutes. Then her door squeaked open and she screamed again, startling a gentleman in an old fedora and bib overalls.

"I just wanted to be sure you were okay," he said.

She grabbed his arm and held on as tears came.

The next day, back at work, she laid her open purse on top of the small sink in the restroom and nervously worked a comb through her thick blonde hair. It had to have been Mickey. God damn him, she thought. She heard he'd been released and Connie's sister had seen him at the Tip Top Lounge over near Jackson. The plan was to be long gone before he got back but like everything else in her life, she'd put it off to the last minute. Now she had no choice - get out of town, the sooner the better. She threw her comb into her purse and pulled out her lipstick, leaned in toward the mirror and steadied her trembling hand. It was the kind of wild stunt that Mickey had been known for. She should have called the cops like the farmer had said. Maybe they'd have put him back in prison. But what if they didn't? He'd come after her for sure. How did she ever get mixed up with a kook like him in the first place?

She slipped the cap back onto the lipstick, dropped it in the purse and checked her face. Of course Mickey wasn't the only one. Somehow she always ended up with the bad boys in the neighborhood. And she had had some fun, some excitement. But what was there to show for it? She was nearly middle-aged and single, a night shift waitress, always broke, and now a busted-up car with a front fender that stuck up higher than the roof. It was time for a quiet guy like that new customer,

Wallace. Wallace didn't know it yet, but she had a plan for him.

He had been crossing the road from the motel when she stepped in to the bathroom. This was the third night he'd been in. They'd talked casually and seemed to get along pretty well. He'd be sliding into the booth by now with his Bible. Connie knew to keep her mitts off. *She* was going to take care of Wallace, and hopefully, when she got done tonight, *he'd* be taking care of her. But she needed to calm down now, needed to forget about last night. She took another deep breath, pushed a thick blonde curl back into place. Not bad for thirty-eight, she thought. She ran her tongue over her teeth and straightened the nametag on her lapel. Her uniform was pink with white trim, a little snug around her hips but okay as uniforms go. The owner of the place, Tony, had insisted on the plunging neckline. "Show a little cleavage, keep the customers happy," he had said.

Wonder what would make Wallace happy, she thought. She studied herself in the mirror. Showing cleavage had never been a problem for her; she had plenty with or without the uniform. She opened her top two buttons and arranged the fabric to reveal glimpses of her bra as she moved in certain ways. "Okay, Wallace," she said. "You may not know it yet, but you're it."

She left the restroom and stashed her purse under the counter. Connie caught her gaze for a moment, motioned toward the booth where Wallace sat reading a menu. Loraine nodded and Connie turned and carried a pot of coffee to the only other customer in the diner.

Wallace returned the menu to the wire holder and flipped through the jukebox selections. Loraine approached the table with her order-pad. "I like *Baby Love* by the Supremes," she said.

Wallace glanced at her. "What's the number?"

"I think it's A22."

He dropped a dime, punched A22. The diner's jukebox came to life with Diana Ross's cooing voice.

"Thanks." Loraine bent slightly forward and put her hand on Wallace's shoulder. "Now I owe you, honey." She smiled as his gaze stopped at her chest. "Nice to see you back. Wallace, right?"

"That's it."

"I've been looking forward to you coming in."

He stared up at her, seemed to roll her words around inside his head. He smiled.

She winked and flipped open her order-pad. "What can I get you?"

"Some coffee, scrambled eggs and toast. That'll do it."

"You got it, honey."

She turned and headed toward the kitchen. In the reflection on a stainless-steel napkin holder she could see him watching her. She stopped, leaned against the counter her back to his booth and

51

pretended to write on her order-pad. Then with one hand she smoothed her uniform over her hip. He continued to watch. She ripped out the page, glanced at him, grinned. She pushed through the double doors into the kitchen. This would be easy.

She brought two cups to the table and poured his coffee. "Mind if I join you? It's almost time for my break and we're pretty slow."

Wallace motioned to the seat with his open hand.

Loraine poured herself a cup and set the glass pot on the Formica table top. She slid into the booth and grabbed two bags of sugar from the condiment rack. She tossed her hair in place with a flip of her head. "Your breakfast won't be but a minute."

Wallace took his coffee black. He sipped as he watched her put in the sugar, stir and then nearly overflow the cup with milk from the stainless steel creamer.

"I don't know how anyone can drink coffee without cream and sugar," she said. She lifted her cup with both hands and stared at him as she pursed her lips and took a sip.

"Why does this place stay open all night?" he said. "It's always dead when I come in."

"We get people off the interstate, some cops and truckers. Shift change at the mill is the crunch time. We were real busy just before you got here."

"That's probably what wakes me up every night."

"Still having trouble sleeping?"

He nodded, yes.

Loraine sipped her coffee again. "You just need something to relax you, honey."

"Yeah?"

"I could help with that."

Wallace stared at her for a moment and then glanced at the Bible resting on the table between them.

Loraine suddenly felt very stupid. She took a sip of her coffee to collect herself.

Wallace picked up the book and put it on the seat next to him. "You were saying?"

She smiled. "Oh, I could get to like you. How much longer are you going to be around?"

"I thought I'd leave in the morning. Maybe head up toward Sault Ste. Marie."

She looked down at her cup. "That soon. I was getting used to you coming in, Wallace." She raised her eyes, locked onto his gaze. "I was hoping we might be able to get to know each other a little better. You know?"

Wallace leaned against the seatback. "Why would you want to get to know me?"

"You seem like a nice guy. The only nice guys around here are married up tighter than a drum."

"Maybe I'm not a nice guy. Maybe I'm a criminal."

"I know some criminals, honey. You're not a criminal."

Wallace stared at her.

Again, Loraine felt uncomfortable but the feeling passed as quick as it had come. Stress from the incident last night, she thought, or her Bible faux pas. Just need to lighten things up. "Well, have you murdered anyone, Wallace?"

He grinned. "No, not today."

"Neither have I. So that's out of the way. Are you happily married?"

Wallace stiffened and looked out the window. "My wife recently passed away."

The words startled her. She lowered her gaze. "Oh. I'm so sorry. I'll stop bugging you." She started to slide out of the booth.

He gently grabbed her arm. "Drink your coffee."

Loraine covered his hand with hers and held on. "That's gotta be hard on you."

"I'm not worried about it."

Just like a man, she thought, probably torn up inside but pretending it doesn't matter. "I'll never be her, but I think you'd like me, Wallace."

"What's not to like?"

She smiled, "See. We're getting to know each other." She squeezed his hand.

A bell sounded in the kitchen. Loraine slid from the booth, went to the pass-through window and picked up his plate of scrambled eggs and toast.

She drank her coffee as Wallace ate his breakfast. She liked how he held his utensils, how he chewed slowly and enjoyed each bite of food. She thought of Mickey, loud, boisterous Mickey, shoveling in his food, his fork clenched in his fist while he talked endlessly and chewed with his mouth open. What a pig. How could she have been such a dope to get caught up in his crazy world? And that awful scene at the trial; he thought she ratted him out. He had come across the rail at her and had to be restrained. Four guards had held him as he lay kicking on the floor, threatening to get her. But it hadn't been her. She had just been called as a witness. She had to tell the truth. What else could she do? Last night's incident overwhelmed her again and she felt a chill.

"So Wallace, what do you do?"

"I'm between jobs. Taking some time off."

"Lucky you. What brings you here?"

"Just getting away, didn't matter where I went."

"Boy, do I know that feeling," Loraine said quietly.

Wallace looked up from his plate.

Loraine leaned against the seatback and folded her arms, hugged off another chill. She needed to stay focused, needed to stop thinking about Mickey and her problems. "It just hasn't been a very good year for me. I'm ready for a change."

Wallace sipped his coffee, then put his elbows on the table and waited for Loraine to go on.

She huffed out a sarcastic laugh. "You see...I'm in a little trouble."

He wrinkled his forehead.

"Money trouble... mostly." She shrugged. "It's not the first time."

"Well, those things work out sooner or later."

"Sooner's what I'm thinking." She picked up the glass pot of coffee and refilled his cup, freshened hers. She smiled. "So you're leaving in the morning?"

Wallace didn't respond.

"If you're not in a rush, if you're flexible," she grabbed his hand and stroked the back of his wrist, "why don't you hang around for another day?" She caught his gaze, held it for a moment. She leaned toward him. "We could have a little fun? It would be good for both of us. "

"How would we have fun?" he said.

She grinned. "Umm, I have my ways, honey. I have my ways."

Connie was trying to check out a customer and having a problem with the cash register. She motioned for Loraine to help.

Loraine slipped from the booth. Wallace's gaze fixed on her ample bosom as she bent down and whispered, "Hold the thought, honey. I'll be right back." Her hair grazed the side of his face as she stood up.

When Loraine finished resetting the register, two state policemen came into the diner. Connie greeted them both by name and directed them to a booth in her section but one of the cops followed Loraine back to Wallace's booth. "Hey, Loraine."

"Hey, Bill. They got you on the nightshift again, huh?" She picked up the coffee pot, and leaned against the seatback.

"Yeah, my turn in the barrel."

Wallace kept his gaze glued to his coffee cup. The cop glanced at him and turned back to Loraine. "What happened to your car?" He motioned toward the parking lot.

Loraine took the pot back to the serving counter. "Some creep ran me off the road on my way home last night."

"Yeah? Who was the investigating officer?"

She waved off his question as the incident began to overwhelm her again. She shook a cigarette from the pack on the counter, lit it and blew out a quick blast of smoke. "Things have been a little rough lately, Bill, financially speaking."

Bill seemed puzzled.

"I might be a little behind on my car insurance premium," she said.

"You get a tag number? Description?"

"All I know is it was an old rusty car with a loud engine. It scared the crap out of me, and whenever I think about it I get scared again, so let's drop it. Okay?"

Bill paused and then nodded. "Okay. I'm glad you're all right." He started toward his table then stopped. "I wouldn't keep driving that around, Loraine. A cop sees you they've got to pull you over. You'll get a ticket and they'll call a tow."

Loraine rolled her eyes.

"Just be careful." Bill turned and walked to his booth in Connie's section.

Loraine leaned against the counter, smoke swirled around her. Life gets better by the minute, she thought. Wallace. She can't blow it now just because of this crap with Mickey and the car. She took another drag, carefully stubbed out the cigarette, and left it on the ashtray for later. She slid back into Wallace's booth, forced a smile.

"Wrecked your car, huh?" Wallace said.

"It's no big deal." She glanced at Connie who was joking with the cops at the other end of the diner. "The bank's going to take it anyway. I got the notice by registered mail yesterday."

Wallace didn't respond.

"Got one from my fat landlady a week before. She gave me thirty days. It's such a crappy place anyway. I ought to report her to the board of health."

"So what are you going to do?"

Loraine shook her head. "I'm leaving, been planning it for months. I've already packed."

"Takes money to pick up and go."

She smiled. "I've got some money. I've been holding back on paying bills and Tony 'll give me my check at the end of the shift today." She shrugged. "I'm okay."

"Where are you going?"

"I don't know. My mother lives out east. I could go there. I haven't decided."

She grabbed Wallace's hand and pouted. "I need to get my mind off things, relax for a while, and you seem like such a sweet guy. What do you say, Wallace?" She stroked his hand. "Stay another day. We can hang out and have a little fun before we go our separate ways."

Wallace pulled his hand free. "I'm not a sweet guy, Loraine."

She paused. Maybe he wasn't a sweet guy, but he was awfully good compared to Mickey. "Honey, in my book you're a double chocolate sundae with whipped cream and candy sprinkles."

He laughed, shifted his gaze to her breasts.

She leaned forward with elbows and forearms on the tabletop. "All yours, baby," she said.

Wallace stared for a moment, then looked out the window at the motel. "What time do you get off?"

"Shift's over at 4:00 am." She glanced at the clock that hung over the pass-through window. "An hour and ten minutes."

A man and woman came into the diner and took the first booth in her section.

"A couple of my regulars just came in. Let me get them going and I'll be back." She smiled at Wallace. "We'll have fun."

She re-buttoned her uniform, took two cups to the regulars and filled them from the glass pot. As she took their orders, she glanced at Wallace who was staring out the window. He's not a bad looking guy, she thought, clean-cut, nice clothes. He's playing a little hard to get, but maybe that's the wife or the religion thing.

She passed the order into the cook. As she approached Wallace's booth, he was startled by something outside. She glanced through the window as two police cruisers rolled to a stop in front of the diner.

She refilled his cup. Four officers came through the door. They walked into Connie's section and talked to Bill and his partner before sitting down in the adjacent booth.

"You do get a lot of cops in here," Wallace said.

"Not this many. Something must be up," she said. An inch of dark coffee sloshed in the bottom of the glass pot. She chewed her thumbnail and thought of Mickey. Maybe he screwed up again. She could only hope.

She turned back to Wallace, her free hand on her hip. "So, we're hanging out when I get done?"

"Seems so."

She made a devilish smile and feigned a shiver. "Ooo. You won't be sorry, Wallace." She leaned close to him and whispered, "Anything you want, baby. You just keep thinking about that." She felt a tingle as she said the words.

He grinned. "I'm going to go back to the motel, room 120, down on the end. My pickup is in front of the door, Missouri plates." He slid from the booth. Loraine momentarily put her hand on his upper arm, then slid the coffee pot on the counter and walked to the register. She pulled out her order-pad, ripped off the check and speared it on a wire post.

"It's five-twenty," she said.

"Give me a pack of those Crystal Lifesavers," he said.

She handed him a roll and made a gagging gesture.

"They're fresh, like you," he said. He put the Bible under his arm, pulled out his wallet and gave her a ten.

She handed him his change. "You haven't seen fresh," she said. "But you will."

61

He dropped two ones on the counter. She picked them up and blew him a kiss as he pushed through the door.

Through the window she watched Wallace tear open the Lifesavers and stroll across the road. Connie came up behind her. "How'd it go?"

"We're playing house after the shift. He still doesn't know he's taking me with him."

"You're moving awfully fast, Loraine. Those Bible thumpers always seem creepy to me."

"He's okay, just a little quiet." She turned toward Connie. "Besides, he's a ticket out of here, and that's what I need right now. If he turns out to be a jerk, I'll find somebody else."

"Just be careful."

Loraine motioned toward the cops. "What's going on?"

"Someone found a body over at Mud Lake. They said there's still a crew at the scene. We'll probably be busy here when they finish up."

"Drowning?"

"No, a homicide. They think it was a hitchhiker."

"Wow. That's big news. "

The bell sounded and Loraine picked up her orders, served her regulars. For the next thirty minutes she swept her section, checked the condiment racks and filled the napkin holders.

At 3:45 am Loraine gasped as Mickey burst through the door in scuffed work-boots, jeans, and an un-tucked flannel shirt. He hadn't shaved in several days and his dirty-blond hair was ragged and unkempt. He smiled, sat down on a stool at the counter and picked up a menu. His gaze remained fixed on Loraine.

Connie approached, pulled out her order-pad. "What can I get you, Mickey?"

Without looking at Connie he said, "I want Loraine to wait on me."

"She's busy," Connie said.

Mickey slapped his hand on the counter. Connie squealed and pulled away as a momentary din of silence filled the diner. Mickey glared and said under his breath, "I want Loraine!"

Bill stood up but Loraine waved him off. "It's okay, Bill. It's okay. I'll take care of it." As she came around the counter she caught the heavy smell of alcohol and tobacco.

"Hey, Loraine. Long time no see." The tip of Mickey's tongue slipped between his stained, slimy teeth. Bill watched for a moment then sat back down.

Loraine folded her arms across her stomach. "What are you doing here?" she said.

"I was in the neighborhood, came by for breakfast, that's all."

"Yeah, well that was some trick last night, Mickey. You could have killed me."

He grinned, opened the menu and scanned the page. "I don't know what you're talking about."

Loraine felt her pulse throbbing in the side of her neck.

Still reading he said, "I see you busted up your car. Too bad." He snapped the menu closed, flipped it onto the countertop.

"Get out of here and leave me alone."

"That's no way to treat a customer, Loraine. What would Tony say?"

"It wasn't me, Mickey. I told you then, and I'm telling you now, it wasn't me."

"Yeah?" He stared at her. His jaw tightened as he gritted his teeth. Loraine caught her breath.

Mickey's expression slowly morphed into a smile. "You're still a fine looking woman, baby." He nodded. "Yeah, I thought of you a lot when I was away. You might say I couldn't get you off my mind."

Loraine clutched her hands against her heart and pleaded, "Mickey, please. You've got to believe me."

He stood. With a finger he twirled the stool and watched till it stopped spinning, then looked up. "I guess I'm not hungry." As he walked away he said, "See you around, Loraine."

With trembling hands Loraine lit the partially smoked cigarette. She took a long drag.

Connie slid onto the stool at the edge of the counter. "What did he say?"

"The bastard! He didn't say anything. He just wanted me to see him. He wanted to scare me." She quickly inhaled another drag and blew out smoke. "And the son of a bitch did a good job."

"Why don't you talk to Bill about it, Loraine?"

She glanced at Bill and then glared at Connie. "What am I going to tell Bill? What could he do?"

"I don't know. Maybe Bill could talk to him; tell him to stay away from you."

"Connie, this is Mickey we're talking about. Cops don't mean anything to him. Don't you think he saw the cars out front before he came in?"

"So what are you going to do?"

Loraine took a last drag and stubbed the cigarette in the ashtray. "What I've been planning to do for the last two months – I'm out of here."

"Well, girl, if I can help you just let me know."

Loraine thought for a moment. "Actually, Mickey is going to be watching for my car so I'm going to leave it out back. Maybe you could ride me around the block and then drop me at the motel so no one spots me walking across the street."

"Sure."

"And if this deal with Wallace falls through I might need you to take me to the bus station. Just keep your fingers crossed that the quiet man likes what he sees."

Connie smiled and held up two crossed fingers.

A half hour later, Loraine took a deep breath and knocked at room 120. The latch clicked from the inside and the door opened. Wallace stood in the doorway wearing pants and a sleeveless undershirt. In the background an old movie played on a black and white TV. With a sweep of his hand, he invited her in.

The room was dingy and small, with a double bed, nightstand, bureau and a plastic chair that looked like it had come from a school cafeteria. The TV sat on a wire cart next to the curtained entrance to the bathroom. The small pillows and threadbare chenille bedspread were wrinkled and askew where Wallace had been lying, watching the movie. A half-full bottle of Coke sat on the floor next to the bed.

The door clicked closed and Wallace threw the latch. Loraine turned and put her arms over his shoulders, pressed against him. She smelled the Crystal Lifesavers. "You been thinking about me, honey?" She kissed him on the side of his neck, her lips lingered. "Hmm?"

Wallace stroked her back, slipped a hand down over the curve of her hip. "Sure, I've been thinking about you."

Loraine smiled and kissed his neck again. "What have you been thinking?" She rubbed against him, waited for his body to respond, for him to speak.

He kissed her on the lips, a quick peck that one might give an old friend. Then he walked to the bed, propped the pillows against the headboard and stretched out as if he were going to watch TV.

What's this? Loraine was momentarily disoriented. Sure, Wallace was a quiet man and maybe a little slow to catch on, but she was practically throwing herself at him. How could he miss that? "You okay, honey?"

"Yeah, I'm fine." He put his arms behind his head and stared at her.

She smiled. "Ah, I bet I know...you want to watch." She moved closer to him and slowly began to unfasten the buttons on her uniform. In a husky voice she asked, "Do you like this, Wallace?" She pulled the dress off her shoulders and down her arms. "Do you like this?"

Wallace stared at her full breasts.

Loraine smiled confidently as she pushed the uniform off her hips and stepped out. Then she pulled down her half-slip and posed in front of him in her bra and panties. She sat down on the bed and began to slowly stroke the inside of his thigh.

"Have you decided what you're going to do?" he said.

God, what's wrong with this guy? She suddenly felt foolish, vulnerable. She folded her arms across her lap and stared at the TV. The Marlboro Man sat on a horse and looked over a placid stream. "What do you mean?"

"Are you serious about leaving town?"

"I quit my job tonight. That's pretty serious." She paused, glanced at the door, felt her plans falling apart and then imagined Mickey's terrifying grin. She shivered. "Connie's going to take me to the bus station when I figure out where I'm going."

His hands still folded behind his head, Wallace said, "Why don't you come with me?"

She spun around and faced him, her eyes wide, mouth open. She put her hands on his chest. Did he just ask her to come with him? "Are you serious?"

"Sure. It would be a blast."

"Oh, Wallace! I'd love to go with you." She laid her head on his chest and hugged him. "You won't be sorry, honey. I'm easy to get along with and I *do* know how to take care of my man." She moved forward and tried to kiss him but he turned his head away and gently pushed her back.

"There'll be time for that. I want to get rolling."

"Oh, honey, but I'm feeling so gushy now." She made a line of kisses down his chest and stomach and with both hands started to stroke the softness in his crotch.

He pushed her away and stood up. "Get dressed and let's go get your stuff. I've already got my bag in the truck." He pulled on his shirt.

As Loraine put her uniform back on Wallace finished buttoning his shirt and pushed the shirttail into his pants. He stood at the window and looked across the road to the diner where another police car pulled into the lot. He took the Lifesavers from his pocket and unpeeled another candy.

Loraine had never been so completely shut down by a man before and she was worried. She had been nearly naked, had had her hands all over him and he didn't respond. No reaction; all business. As she buttoned her uniform she thought, this could be a problem. She couldn't be with a man that didn't have needs, or wouldn't react to hers. What kind of life would that be? But he *was* taking her away; she *was* getting what she wanted. And that's a very good thing, and for now at least, would have to do. Maybe the next time, when Mickey was a thousand miles away, things would be better. They could take their time.

As they pulled away from the motel Loraine turned in her seat and scanned the diner's lighted parking lot.

"Every time you look there's another cop over there," Wallace said.

Loraine settled back. "There's an investigation going on over at Mud Lake."

"Oh yeah?"

"They found a body."

When Wallace didn't respond Loraine turned and looked at him. He thumbed a lifesaver off the roll and slipped it into his mouth.

At the trailer, Loraine opened the door to get out of the truck. She looked at Wallace. "Aren't you going to come in?"

He stared at her a moment before answering. His voice was different, his words slower than usual. "You said you were packed. I'll just wait here."

Loraine stepped down onto the dirt driveway. "Okay, but it will take me a few minutes to change and get my cosmetics together."

Wallace nodded, took a deep breath. "Take your time."

She started to close the door but hesitated. "Everything okay, honey?"

He stared at her again. "Yes," he finally said.

Maybe I've been smart to avoid the quiet guys, she thought as she walked up the trailer's iron steps. She slipped the key into the door and realized this would be the last time she ever saw this crummy old place again. She took the key off her key-ring and it clattered onto the kitchen table. She put her purse on the counter, flipped on the hall light and started toward the bedroom.

As she passed the bathroom, a strange odor reminded her of Mickey, how he reeked of alcohol and tobacco, and then hands gripped her tightly around the neck and she was pushed from behind, smashed through the bedroom door and onto the unmade bed.

She gasped as a heavy knee pressed her down and Mickey's breathless voice snarled, "Hello Loraine! I'm so fucking glad you made it home all right."

She couldn't move, couldn't breathe. She choked, gurgled and clutched at the muscular fingers digging into her throat.

"I see you've been packing. Are you going away, Loraine? You taking a little trip? I thought maybe you'd have a welcome home party for me." He released his grip on her throat, but clamped a hand on the back of her neck, pushed down, and grabbed a fistful of hair.

Pressed into the mattress and unable to speak, Loraine gasped for breath.

"Maybe I should break your neck, baby. I hear it's the best way to kill a rat."

Suddenly Mickey's grip went soft and he crumpled onto her. She pushed herself up and his body slumped to the floor. From the glow of the hall light, Wallace's silhouette loomed behind her, a large hammer hanging from his hand.

Mickey groaned and his body writhed on the floor. Wallace bent over and swung the hammer again. A dull thud sounded and Mickey's legs stiffened, quivered. Wallace swung again. Another dull thud and the hammer stuck in Mickey's skull. Wallace jerked the hammer until it came loose.

Loraine couldn't speak and was gasping for breath, but she waved her hand at Wallace to make him stop. With one arm she held herself in a sitting position. She coughed and choked; tears started. In the partial light she saw a growing semi-circle of blood oozing through the carpet around Mickey's head.

Wallace stared at the body for several seconds then dropped the hammer and sat down on the bed next to her. He took her in his arms. She cried on his shoulder, still barely able to breathe. He rubbed her back.

Her throat hurt and her back was sore where Mickey had kneeled on her. It hurt to cry, but she couldn't stop. God, what if he *had* broken her neck? How lucky that Wallace had been nearby. She tightened her arms around him and he rocked her back and forth.

She peeked at the body and then closed her eyes, buried her face in Wallace's chest as if that might make everything go away, make it like it didn't happen. Wallace slipped his hand up her dress and stroked her bottom over her nylon panties. Loraine stiffened, unsure of what was happening. She tried to speak but her bruised throat caused her to choke instead. Wallace took a deep breath then rolled her onto the bed and ran his hand up and down her crotch. She coughed, held up her hand for him to stop and then tried to get up but he pushed her down and with both hands pulled her panties off. She coughed again, tried to say not now, but the words wouldn't come. He undid his pants, slid them to his knees. "This is what you wanted, isn't it?" he said as he crawled on top of her. "So it shall be."

Not now, she thought. Not now.

Later, as they drove out of town a sliver of light crept across the eastern sky and the evening's darkness began to fade. Wallace pulled another Lifesaver from the roll and slipped it in his mouth. Loraine sat zombie-like in the passenger seat unable to shake the image of Mickey on the blood-soaked carpet.

Wallace's Bible lay on the seat between them. He unconsciously stroked the cover with his fingers.

"How did you know he was there?" Loraine asked.

"I didn't," he said. "I'd come in for you." He turned and stared at Loraine then looked back to the road. "To help you."

Nothing was making sense to her. Where did the hammer come from? Maybe Mickey... Mickey, all she could see was his limp body, the blood spreading.

Wallace flipped on the radio. Tammy Wynette sang *Stand by Your Man*.

For the first time Loraine noticed the rubber covered handle of the hammer leaning against the seat between them. She quickly looked away, closed her eyes and put her fingers on her forehead. "Why'd you bring that thing?" She shook her head in exasperation. "This is awful! They're going to think I did it," she said. "They're going to find him and come after me."

Wallace kept his eyes on the road. "They'll know it wasn't you," he said.

Loraine shook her head and then massaged her temples. How can he say that? God, what a morning this has been. Suddenly she twisted in her seat and frantically searched the cab of the truck. "Where are my bags? Did you get my bags?"

Wallace spoke slowly. "They're in the back."

Loraine looked through the back window. "Where?"

"They're there," he said.

Loraine slumped down in her seat and listened as Tammy finished the song. A booming, echoing commercial for a car dealership followed, and then a DJ read a news bulletin:

"State Police report that a body has been found in a rural area just outside Mud Lake in Jackson County. While investigators are still on the scene and details are limited, the spokesman reports that this has been designated as a homicide investigation. The victim was a U.S. serviceman."

This is what the cops at the diner were talking about, she thought. That seems like it was years ago.

"Mr. Marley Norris, a local resident, had been scavenging for aluminum cans late yesterday afternoon when he discovered the body and reported it to police. Norris said the man was partially clothed and had been bludgeoned to death.

"Police request..."

Wallace turned off the radio.

More visions raced through Loraine's head. Partially clothed, bludgeoned to death? Without moving her head, Loraine glanced at the hammer and then quickly shifted her gaze out the side window. Her imagination went totally out of control. Calm down, she told herself. I've got to stop this! And then she blurted, "Oh, Wallace, I'm scared. What's going to happen to me?"

Wallace stroked the Bible. "Nothing to worry about, Loraine," he said in a steady voice. "The Lord has a plan for us all."

POSTSCRIPT

A week later, Wallace checked out of a motel outside of Chillicothe, Ohio. He hung Rhonda's silver necklace over his rearview mirror and pinned Loraine's nametag onto the chain. He put the sailor's hat on the seat next to his Bible and dropped in the razor, a watch with a Chrysler logo, and a turtle-shell barrette he had acquired the night before.

He thought about the young redhead, how her hair had spilled across her cheek in waves after he had removed the barrette. He picked it up again, remembering every moment, every glorious sensation. He shuddered, closed his eyes and held the barrette to his lips.

A few moments later, Wallace slipped the key into the ignition and started the engine. He backed out of the parking space and headed toward the exit, wondering which way he should go.. He could drive south on Route 23 and spend some time in the Lexington area, then maybe head on over to Nashville. But he could just as easily go east to Charleston.

Wherever he went there would be plenty for him to do.

Notes and Acknowledgements

"The Hitchhiker" first appeared in the January 2012 edition of *Crimespree Magazine*. This story also won 2nd place in the short-story category of the Delaware Press Association's 2013 communications contest.

"Abracadabra" first appeared in the anthology, *Someone Wicked,* published in 2013 by Smart Rhino Publications.

My thanks to the members of my writing group – Bob Davis, Barbara Gray, Ramona Long and Maggie Rowe – for honest critiques and for their support over the years. I have been so fortunate to be included in this group of fine writers.

And thanks to the many teachers, workshop leaders and brilliant writers I have met throughout my writing career. Their almost universal willingness to help and share has been invaluable and a great inspiration to me. Thank you all.

ABOUT THE AUTHOR

Russell Reece grew up in Wilmington, Delaware and served in the Navy's amphibious force during the Vietnam War. Since 2003, he has had stories, essays, and poems published in numerous print and on-line journals. His work has also appeared in anthologies, most recently *All That Glitters*, published by Lominy Books, and *Someone Wicked,* published by Smart Rhino Publications, both released in 2013. He has received two Best of the Net nominations and was a finalist in the 2012 William Faulkner/ William Wisdom Creative Writing Contest. Russ is a University of Delaware alumnus. He lives in rural Delaware, near Bethel, along the beautiful Broad Creek. You can learn more about Russ by visiting his website at russellreece.com.